Befriending the Beast

Amanda Hew
Prov 3:5-7

Befriending the Beast

Amanda Tero

Befriending the Beast

© 2016 by Amanda Tero

Published by Amanda Tero
Decatur, MS 39327

All Scripture references taken from the King James Version. Public domain.

This novel is a work of fiction. The characters in this story are fictitious. Any resemblance to persons living or dead is coincidental.

ISBN: 978-1-942931-19-5

Cover design by Amanda Tero
Images from
    www.pixabay.com
Used by permission.

Formatted by Amanda Tero

To Aimee Hebert

Because you sure do put up with a lot of me!
- your beloved "sandpaper."

Chapter One

Belle wasn't sure she was ready to return. But she knew it was time. She sank back into the plush red cushions of the carriage and took a deep breath to steady her nerves. The next second, she leaned forward to stare out the window. The scenery should look familiar by now, yet it didn't. But then, didn't things change with time?

Time. Belle leaned back again and closed her eyes. Had Papa changed any? How would he take her return? Should she have written? She doubted it would have done any good. Unless... dare she hope that he was different now?

"Whoa!" The carriage slowed, then jerked, as it came to a complete stop. Whether or not she was ready, Belle was home.

The door opened, and the footman held his hand out to Belle. She slipped her gloved hand into his and climbed down. The coachmen moved her trunks from the carriage to the ground. If Belle hadn't been so desperate to come home today—so worried that someone would hinder her from returning here—Anis would have been with her, seeing to her things. However, the morrow would come soon enough, with her lady-in-waiting and the rest of her belongings.

Her hands burrowed into the full skirt of her brown gown, the handfuls of fabric soothing her. *I can do this.* Her quivering body seemed to disagree as she forced herself to look at the castle she had left behind years ago. The front walls protruded on either side of the double doors, as if guarding the entrance. Towers rose on the sides of the castle, making her feel small and insignificant.

"Your royal highness."

Belle turned to the coachman, who bowed before her with his arm held out. She slid her hand into the crook of the man's arm as he escorted her towards the castle. Her slow steps rustled her dress as she moved forward. The doors in front of her swung open, and a young butler stepped out.

"May I help you, miss?" he asked stiffly.

The coachman straightened as he eyed the butler. "I present to you her royal highness, Princess Belle, daughter of the king."

The butler's poise matched the coachman's. He gave Belle a stiff bow, eyeing her with doubt. "His majesty has not mentioned that he is expecting your royal highness' return."

"Nay, he isn't expecting me." Belle pitied the butler, who seemed torn between his duties toward the king and the princess presented at the castle doors. "May I speak with Geoffrey? Or—or Isabel?" She cringed. Lady Kiralyn would frown at her lack of confidence.

"Come with me." The butler bowed again, then looked at the coachman. "You may place her trunks in the front passage."

Belle followed the butler through the corridor and into the drawing room.

Here, in the absence of the coachman, the butler lifted his head, looking down his nose at her. "One moment." His voice was haughty as he left Belle in silence.

How many years had it been since she had last stood here? Six or seven at least. Standing here, though, time faded. She walked to the window and looked out. The grounds were immaculate. Trees sprinkled the front lawn, bushes hedged the circular drive, everything was trimmed and neat, just as it had been when she had left.

"Your highness?" the voice behind her sounded more hesitant than surprised.

Belle spun around. "Isabel!" She half-ran to the maid then paused slightly before gently clasping her arms.

"Let me have a look!" Isabel stepped back. "Why did you not send word? Your room isn't freshened up! Ack! Child, you are beautiful! Favian, order her things in."

The two slipped past the butler and into the front hall.

"Is—is Papa well?" Belle asked, her voice low.

Isabel shrugged her shoulders. "Has the royal beast—beg pardon." The apology wasn't sincere. "Has his majesty ever been well since..." Her gaze slipped from Belle's and she shifted her weight.

Belle sighed. "'T'was wrong of me to stay away."

"Tsk!" Isabel led Belle towards the stairs. "That did not make him become the man he is today."

Belle stopped walking and stared at the maid, who continued making her way up the stairs. What had Papa become? She didn't follow Isabel, but paused at the foot of the staircase and looked around. The front room was large and empty. She remembered days past when it would be lit and filled with the chatter of happy people. Today, the only brightness came from the sunlight which dared to peek out from among the drapes. Her footsteps sounded empty... hollow... as she turned to follow Isabel.

"Where is your lady-in-waiting?" Isabel demanded when Belle joined her.

"Do not fret," Belle raised her hand, the long, silky sleeve falling down to her elbow. "She shall be here on the morrow. I did not wish to wait."

"The morrow!" Isabel shook her head, her brows furrowed. "Plunging headlong into things still."

"I try to do better." Belle lowered her voice. "Has Papa dismissed all the servants?" Things were too quiet around the castle.

"Dismissed…" Isabel shrugged. "Some fled. Only a few of us remain here."

"Why didn't you go?"

"Tsk! Don't mind my words. I only half mean what I say. Some things cannot be forgotten." Isabel's voice faded to a whisper as she added, "Or some people."

Belle nodded. Mama had been the essence of beauty. The life of the castle. The gentle hand in the midst of trouble. No one could ever forget her.

"Here we are!" There was a hint of cheer in Isabel's voice.

Though the room was dark, the pale blue walls sent a wave of memories over Belle. She wanted to stay and relax here, letting the memories wash over her.

"I can have my things moved into the room adjoining yours, if you wish." Isabel's stern glance spoke of her disapproval for Belle's solitude. Belle was certain the maid would move into the next room, even if she said she did not wish it. "I'll direct your things up here," Isabel said, leaving Belle alone in the silence.

Belle laid a hand on the Persian blue bedspread. She could barely see the colors, but she knew this place well. It had been her quiet escape. She walked towards the window and pulled back the heavy curtain, sending a shaft of light into the chamber. One glance told her that these gardens, too, had remained the same. She looked up to the sky. "Lord, I'm here." Urgency surged through her being. "Please show me what to do."

Chapter Two

$\mathcal{B}$elle stood in front of the clock and stared at the motionless hands. "At what hour do we dine?" she asked, as if the timeless clock would help her to know when the hour was approaching. She would have to find someone to fix it.

"We haven't a dinner hour," Isabel answered curtly as she pulled clothes from Belle's trunk. In the time that they had been up here, Isabel had whisked around, dusting, changing bed sheets, and opening drapes, barely stopping between tasks.

"Why not?"

"His majesty prefers to eat alone. and when he pleases. Are you ready for dinner, your highness?"

"Aye." Belle turned from the clock as Isabel hung the last of Belle's gowns—the fabric was an airy pink that Lord Kiralyn, Belle's uncle, had chosen for her.

"Prepare for wagging tongues, your highness." Isabel gave a grunt as she opened the door. "Favian has likely told the whole castle that you have arrived."

Belle kept silent as she let Isabel guide her, though she hadn't forgotten her way to the kitchen. She would let Isabel treat her as a guest today.

As they hurried through the halls and rooms, Belle snatched glimpses of the faded grandeur. Heavy curtains kept the sun from sending rays of brightness into the rooms, draping them all in somber darkness.

They neared the kitchen before Belle realized that they had not passed a single soul. How many servants had been dismissed or, as Isabel put it, had fled? An empty castle seemed ill-advised, even if this was a time of peace.

Scents from the kitchen greeted Belle as they descended the final flight of steps. Welcome light spilled out from a large stone oven in the middle of the room. Tables lined the walls, with half-empty barrels and buckets underneath. Used to be, Belle would slip into the kitchen and hide in the corner. There was always much motion with the skirts of busy maids swishing around as they paid her no mind. Today, only one younger maid walked about. Someone Belle didn't remember.

"Serve up a dish for the princess," Isabel commanded, joining the maid in her work.

"Yes, ma'am." The maid barely glanced up from peeling carrots. Her head bobbed towards Belle in a slight bow as she quickened her speed.

"Oh, you needn't hurry on my account," Belle said. "What is your name?"

"Grede, your highness."

"You must be new, like Favian."

A faint tint of pink brushed Grede's cheeks. "Yes, your highness." Her blue eyes peeked up at Belle before dropping again to watch her hands.

Quick, steady footsteps interrupted the silence that had fallen.

"His majesty demands—" Percy stopped short as he surveyed Belle. His heels clicked together and he gave a low bow. His voice softened as he said, "Your highness, my pleasure to see you again."

"The pleasure is mine, Percy." Belle held out her hand to the middle-aged scribe.

A fond smile played at Percy's lips. He glanced at Grede. "A plate for the King. And he is not patient."

"Is he ever?" Isabel muttered. Percy shot her a cold glare.

"How is my father?" Belle walked over to Percy and looked up at him. His hair was almost completely gray, just traces of dark brown remaining.

Percy's face tensed. "I'm afraid he is not pleased with your unannounced return."

15

"Would he have been pleased if it were announced?"

Percy shook his head. "I wish I could say he would be." He took the tray Grede had prepared. He walked out of the doorway then paused. "Your highness..." He turned back towards Belle, but didn't make eye contact.

"Yes, Percy?"

"The king refuses to see you."

Belle nodded. "I understand his eve may be full, and did not expect him to—"

"Nay," Percy shook his head solemnly. "Not ever."

Chapter Three

*D*ark stillness surrounded Belle. Though her body sank into the fluffiness of the bed, she couldn't relax. Isabel's snores from the next room assured her that the hour for sleep should have come a long time ago. Slipping out of bed, Belle crept across the cool marble floor to the window. Only a sliver of the moon showed its face tonight.

Belle slid onto the window seat and pulled her legs towards her, resting her chin on her knees. For a moment, she stared into the darkness, the conversation she'd overheard a few weeks ago playing in her mind. She had been in the sitting room of her aunt and uncle's, buried in the world of reading. She hadn't intended on eavesdropping, but Lord and Lady Kiralyn's voices were easily heard from the next room.

"Something must be done with the girl." Belle's uncle sounded agitated. "She is, all things considered, our child now. But if we do not do things properly, we could be beheaded."

"He isn't so brutal, my lord."

"Whatever the case is, 'tis near time for Belle to make her debut. She is too lovely to be left in the shadows. And 'tisn't fitting for the lineage to cease because her father refuses to take part in her life. If she *were* my own daughter—and I daresay that she is more mine than Jarin's—I would do everything in my power to fit her for her position."

"But you know we should do nothing without the king's assent."

"Aye, I just said that." Lord Kiralyn had an impatient growl in his voice. "We shall see about getting her father to transfer guardianship over to us by her sixteenth birthday. Jarin cannot disannul her royalty, even with us as her guardians."

Belle's book slipped to the floor unnoticed as she stood. As a child, she had fled to her aunt and uncle's to escape the sorrows of Mama's passing and found their arms open wide. But did these same arms seek to forever separate her from Papa? If she were still the eight-year-old weeping over her father's grief, she might be grateful for Lord Kiralyn's interference. But things had changed this winter. Beyond her understanding, she felt the yearning to go back. Her uncle's declaration to contact Papa changed her yearning into a firm decision.

Lord, tonight, she couldn't bring her lips to speak, *I thought Thou leddest me here to try again. But if Papa refuses to see me, how can I tell him I'm sorry? How can I make up for leaving him alone like that? Please show me the next step to take.*

Dim light played on her face as she turned to wordless prayer, trusting that her Lord, Who saw her heart, knew what it was crying though she was unable to utter it.

"Your highness!" Reproof etched Isabel's voice as she laid a firm hand on the princess.

Belle looked up and squinted in the morning brightness.

"Was your bed not to your liking? Has Lady Kiralyn spoilt you to where your own comfortable bed is detestable?"

"Nay." Belle yawned and rubbed her eyes. "Auntie Elayne's palace may not be quite so fine, but 'twasn't the bed that kept me from sleeping."

Isabel huffed as she pulled out a gown for Belle.

"Something simple today, please." If Anis was here, she would know the proper dress for Belle. But it would be mid-morn before the lady-in-waiting arrived.

Isabel returned the laced emerald dress for a slender, cream dress with gold trim and helped her into it.

"I'm sorry I came ahead of Anis. I didn't realize this would hinder your work."

"Tsk!" Isabel's fingers ran through Belle's hair as she prepared to braid it. "Your coming has broken the dullness of the days here."

When her hair was finished, Belle went down the stairs. This time, she would take the walk to the kitchen more leisurely. The first room she came to was the ballroom. As a child, she remembered dances and festivities in this room. The chandeliers would have been lit, reflecting brilliantly off the golden arches that accented the ceiling. Now, it was dark and dreary.

With a shiver, she left the room behind and hurried through the back corridor, slipping past the other rooms. The stone steps to the kitchen made her footsteps echo as she rushed down.

"Good morn, your highness." Grede's voice had a slight bounce to it as she greeted the princess. "May I fix your breakfast?"

"Yes, please."

"What shall it be?"

"What have you prepared?"

"Nay, your highness." Grede laughed. "You tell me, and I shall prepare it."

"Well, then." Belle found a stool to sit on.

Grede's brows furrowed, "Your highness, I can call Favian to bring more than a stool for you to sit upon. We are not accustomed to royalty gracing our kitchen."

Belle shook her head. "I may be the princess, but Lady Kiralyn taught me to never frown upon what is available."

"Very well, your highness." Grede paused and looked timidly at Belle. "You still have not told me your desire."

Belle laughed. "I shall take bread and cheese."

"What? A peasant's fair?" Grede brought her hand to her chest and her cheeks flushed a darker pink. "With all respect, your highness."

"You asked what I wanted, there 'tis."

"Aye, your highness. May I add herring or—or beef to that fare? Milk, surely."

"I assure you, bread and cheese—with the milk— shall be fine. I'm not one for eating much in the morn."

"Aye, your highness." Grede began preparations swiftly. "Shall I take it to the dining hall?"

"Nay." Belle shuddered at the thought of breakfasting alone in the large, empty room that used to seat her and her family. "Do you enjoy work here, Grede?"

"'Tis as well as any place. Though 'tis pleasant to have direct orders for meals instead of fixing a meal only to have it returned." Grede looked shyly at Belle. "No disrespect to his majesty." She leaned in and whispered, "Would you know that I have worked here for a full year and have yet to see him thrice?"

"I see," Belle said. "Percy has always run the errands he's needed, and meals must be one of those errands." As she assured Grede, she grew more confused. Had Papa grown into a complete recluse, seeing no one? Percy would know the answer.

As soon as her breakfast was finished, Belle asked, "Has Papa breakfasted yet?"

"Nay, your highness. Percy has not yet come."

"Thank you."

Belle retraced her steps to the second floor. A dozen bedchambers separated Belle's room from the king's suite. As she walked through the passage, the length made her heart sink. Before Mama had gotten sick, Belle's chamber was adjacent to Papa and Mama's. She would sneak past her nursemaid at night when she was scared and crawl into bed with them. Papa had let her wander into his study and sit by him quietly when he did his business. At first, Belle's room had been moved so she would not disturb Mama, but after Mama died, Papa didn't seem to care that

Belle's room was moved. Instead, she felt forbidden from that end of the castle.

Today, however, she needed some answers. And the best way to find Percy was to go to Papa's end of the castle. Though it had been years since Belle had braved coming this close, her memory filled in the view behind closed doors. The door to her left was the bedchamber. The one at the end of the hall was Papa's study. One day, Belle was going to enter it again. Or so she hoped and prayed.

Muffled voices came from behind the door. Belle shifted her weight as her body shuddered against her will. What would Papa say if he saw her standing in the hall? She took a few steps back until her body pressed against the stone wall. The voices grew louder. Then it was just one voice. Shouting. The door muddled the diction of the words, but the tone was clear.

Belle covered her face with her hands. *Lord, I don't know what to do here. This is beyond me. I—*

The shouting suddenly became clear and Belle peeked through her fingers. The door had opened and she could hear each word of the argument.

"This! This is what your—your meddling has wrought!"

"But your—"

"Leave!" the king roared the word and something crashed against the wall.

Percy emerged from the room, and the door slammed behind him. His mouth was set in a firm line despite his shoulders sagging. He took a quick breath then straightened his shoulders and marched forward.

Belle stepped away from the wall.

Percy's eyes narrowed when he saw her. "I advise you to never come here again." His words were short and rapid, matching his steps as he passed Belle.

"Was he talking of me?" Belle hurried to catch up with Percy. "Will Papa—will he send you away… because of me?"

Percy stopped. "Nay, he would never send me away. There is no one else he trusts." The words had a sorrowful tinge lacing them. "Do not worry yourself of the king's matters."

"But I am his daughter."

"Aye…" Percy sighed and resumed walking, his pace slower as he thought. "Mayhap there are seasons in which it would be wise to occupy your time elsewhere than the castle."

"Have seven years not been sufficient?"

"Just give him more time."

Belle stopped and let Percy continue without her. More time? There were three months to convince Papa to let her stay. And if he refused, then these were her last three months in the castle. How sufficient was that time?

Chapter Four

Delightful fragrance flittered through the air as the wind brushed scent from the herb leaves. Peppermint, basil, dill, cilantro, and thyme were creatively planted amidst squash, tomatoes, onions, peas, green beans, and other vegetables. The kitchen garden had never really attracted Belle, but it was a part of home. A part of her life which might soon be abolished.

Leaving the small garden behind, Belle traipsed through the intricate knot garden. They were exquisite, just as Olli had always kept them—if he was even master of the grounds still.

Birds whistled pleasantly around her, chasing each other through the various trees and bushes as if trying to convince Belle that somber life lived only inside of the castle. The gentle splashing of the fountain and distant sound of the horses from the stables joined in the harmony of the birds' music; the songs of the castle grounds that Belle loved.

Today, the songs only served to bring Belle back. Back to a time when they were a happy family. When Mama had planned her rose garden, inviting Belle to select her favorite roses to embellish the plot. When deer had threatened the garden, Papa ordered walls to be built around it, creating what he called their secret garden. Many times, it was just Belle and Mama inside, leaving the world with its cares and sorrows shut out.

A burning desire for this serenity overtook Belle, and she rushed around the walls until she reached the gate. Vines wove in and out of the intricate ironwork, creating a shield that blocked Belle's view of the flowers inside. She reached for the latch. A lock was rusted onto it. The garden had never been locked before. Pulling at the vines, she created a hole big enough to peek inside. Her heart, which had quickened in pace, now seemed to skip a beat. Only a few tall canes stood bravely amidst the tangle of weeds, the stems dropping with the remainders of flowers that had bloomed, dried up, and died. The paths and garden beds were hidden by brambles, nothing like the paradise she remembered.

Footsteps sounded behind Belle and she spun around, schooling her face to be calm. A stranger stood in front of her.

"You must be the gardener," Belle guessed. It certainly was not Olli.

The older man before her gave a low bow. "Aye, your highness. Carpus, at your service."

"Carpus." Belle turned and fingered the lock. "Is there a key to this gate?"

A look of alarm crossed Carpus' face then disappeared. "It has been locked since before I was here, your highness."

"No one enters it?"

"Nay, your highness."

"Why not?"

Carpus glanced at the castle then looked back to Belle. "Percy told me it was his majesty's orders. And I am not one to question the king's demands."

Belle swallowed her torrent of questions and gave Carpus a stiff smile. "Thank you, Carpus."

"My pleasure, your highness." Carpus bowed again then hurried to resume his tasks.

Belle turned back to the garden, clinging to the memories that seemed to be corroding quickly. There was one place left to visit. Another place where the past had been pleasant. Bracing herself, Belle left the gardens behind. A long, empty field spanned in front of her, the grass bright green. How was it possible for everything outside to be bright and cheery, yet her heart feel so heavy and sorrowful?

At the crest of the field rested the large stables. It was dwarfed compared to the castle, but Belle knew that it was one of the finest stables in the country.

The side door was easy to open and the nutty smell of hay rushed over Belle. She plunged into the dimness of the stables and stood, surveying the rows of empty stalls in silence.

"Good morn," a bright, cheery voice greeted. "You must be the long-lost princess. My pleasure." The man swooped into a low bow.

"I am. And you are…?"

"Linus, your highness." Another bow. "How may I help my lovely princess?"

"I am..." What was she doing here? Trying to relive her past? Grasping for any promise that life hadn't changed? "Does Papa still own Keirstrider?"

"Aye." A broad grin spread across Linus' face. "Still rides him every day. Keeps him in the stall nearest the pasture. Follow me, your highness."

There he was, in a secluded stall. His large head hovered over the door, golden hair sweeping over his forehead. Belle stepped past Linus and held out her hand to Keirstrider.

"'Tis good to see you again, Keir," Belle spoke softly as Linus stepped away.

Keirstrider's soft nose touched Belle's hand. At the invitation, Belle threaded her fingers in Keirstrider's mane, letting her palms rest on his golden neck. She lowered her forehead until it touched the white star on Keirstrider's head. She squeezed her eyes shut, keeping tears from sliding down her cheeks. Here, with Papa's treasured horse, she felt near him. Much nearer than when she had heard his voice screaming at Percy.

"Keir, I miss him," she whispered, not sure the horse could hear her low murmur. "If only you could talk. Then, in the morn when he rides you, you could give him that message." She pulled away and looked into the old horse's blue eyes. The horse blinked slowly and Belle backed away then fled from the stables.

Chapter Five

If there is a key to the garden, your father has it."
Percy offered the information slowly as he pulled several
books from the bookcase.

"Could you ask him for it, since he refuses to
see me?"

"Nay." Percy shook his head. "There are some things
even I don't ask for." He stacked the books on the side
table before reaching for more.

"Would it be wrong for me to enter the garden, if I
found a way?" Belle laid a hand on Percy's arm. Finding
Papa's books was only his pretense to brush her off, and
she knew it.

Percy stopped his search and sighed. "His majesty
ordered it locked."

"Aye, and…?"

"I have heard nothing of the garden being expressly
forbidden." He must have noticed her eyes light up,

because he hastened to add, "Locking the garden is akin to forbidding it, your highness."

Belle motioned to the settee in the center of the library. "Please, be seated, Percy. I need some answers."

Percy hesitated, tilted his head in a bow, then sat next to Belle. "I am not certain I have answers, your highness."

"Have all of the original servants left? That is, besides you and Isabel?"

"Aye."

"Are the only other servants Grede, Favian, Carpus, and Linus?"

"Aye."

"Why so few?" Belle studied Percy as he paused before answering. "Please, Percy, tell me."

"Very well then." Percy stood and began pacing in front of Belle. "When your mother died, it seemed to take a part of his majesty. It was as if she was the reason for his living. I think you are a part of that memory of Queen Ryia. And the king has yet to accept that she is no longer here—and, that his life is not just about himself."

Belle nodded, knowing that Percy meant no disrespect for his master. "What has Papa been doing these past few years?"

"That, your highness, I cannot satisfactorily answer." Percy frowned. "He has his duties, I assure you, yet beyond those, he occupies his time doing little to nothing. If it is unnecessary for him to be seen, then I attend his callers."

Silence hung between them. What could be said when nothing had changed for the past decade?

"The kingdom is indebted to your faithfulness to my father. I am grateful."

The pacing stopped and Percy stood before Belle, his hands clasped behind his back. "Why did you return?"

"I've not yet put it into words." Belle took a deep breath as her reasons flooded her. Even Percy could not know the pressure of why she chose to return yesterday. "'Tis—'tis hard to know where to begin."

Percy took the seat next to Belle again. "Very well. Begin at the beginning." He smiled encouragingly.

Belle closed her eyes for a moment. "It was this past winter. We were at the church for Christmas service." She opened her eyes, tears suddenly forming. "Mama always liked Christmas, so it has been special for me because of that."

Percy reached over and patted her hand.

"There is something so beautiful about the season. Children are happy, parents are smiling. Something connects them all.

"This Christmas eve, there was a new friar. He explained the story of the Christ-child. I have heard it since infanthood. This time, however, he asked us why we still celebrated Christ's birth, since it happened so long ago. I didn't know the answer." Belle reached in her pocket and drew out a small, gilded book. "Percy, do you know the answer?"

The older man smiled. "Mayhap, but I shall be pleased to hear it from the princess' lips."

"Jesus is the Son of God. And in heaven, He is surrounded by royalty and grandeur—far greater than anything I have seen on this earth. And yet He left it all so that He could take the sins of the world to the cross, and die in our place. You see, the wages of sin—any sin, great or small—is death. And that payment must be made.

"I must admit," Belle lowered her head, "I love the fancy things that surround my life, and if some wretch were to die for his transgressions, I certainly would not leave my position, like Jesus did, to take his place. A wretch does not deserve it."

When Belle paused, Percy asked, "And the story ends there?"

"Nay." Belle gave a slight laugh. "You may think it childish, but I had lied to Auntie—Lady Kiralyn—the week before. Something frivolous and silly, but I had convinced myself that no harm was done. During the friar's speech, however, all of the 'small' sins I committed piled up until I realized the truth about myself: I was a sinner. Just like any wretch, I should die for my transgressions. I was not perfect and thus could not enter God's perfect heaven. Being a princess did not make my sins better than a peasant's sins.

"The friar said that God's Spirit works in our hearts to convict us of sin. He explained that if we respond to this, if we repent from our sins and accept that Jesus Christ is the only way to heaven, then He will forgive us our sins." Belle's face blossomed into a smile. "Percy, I did just that." A look of peace and joy came over Percy's face at those words. Belle clasped his hands in her excitement. "You've known Jesus Christ as your Savior for a while yet, have you not?"

"Aye, your highness." Percy's large hands patted Belle's in a fatherly fashion. "And I am praising the Lord that He has you in the fold too."

"Auntie Elayne said that Mama was saved—and for the first time since her death, I have such peace, because I know that I shall see her again."

The happiness in Belle's eyes faded as she looked down the darkened halls that led away from the parlor. "It was that same night that I thought of Papa again." She looked ashamed. "I had done my best to forget him and convince myself that I no longer cared. But that night, I cared." Her throat tightened and she fought back tears. "And since then, I couldn't stop thinking about Papa. I know he's not the same as when Mama was alive. I lived with him for a few years and saw the change, but I wondered if things were different now."

Percy shook his head solemnly. "Nay, your highness. I fear he has gotten worse."

Belle took a quivering breath. "For months I fought it, but I knew that the Lord was telling me to come back home. I still don't know why. If Papa refuses to see me, and if my return has angered him, what good does it do?" If Lord Kiralyn desired to adopt her, would she be better off to just leave? What would being here for only a few short months merit? She whispered her fears aloud. "Is there any hope?"

Percy squeezed her fingers gently. "Only time will tell. We shall keep praying, aye?"

Belle nodded. "Aye." She could pray fervently for Papa, but time was the one thing she didn't have.

Chapter Six

$\mathcal{B}$elle fingered the rusted lock, the lock that kept her from her paradise on earth. That kept her from the one place she felt like she needed to be today. Her fingers slipped down to the pocket of her blush pink dress, brushing against the letter hidden beneath the folds.

Seeing Carpus in the distance, Belle lifted her skirts and ran towards him. "Carpus!" She hoped the tremor in her voice came from running, not from the emotions bottled up inside of her.

The man stood up straight then bowed. "Your highness," he called as he took several strides towards her. "How may I assist you this morn?"

"I desire access into the garden."

Carpus looked over his shoulder at the castle and lowered his voice. "I am not certain such is a good idea."

Belle followed his gaze to the dark windows. Papa's room was on this side of the castle, but she had studied his window for hours. Only once did she think the curtain moved. And that may have been her imagination.

"Percy said that Papa hasn't expressly forbidden it." She paused. The letter seemed to weigh heavily in her pocket, urging her to that one place where she could shut out these sorrows. "Have you any idea how to enter?"

Carpus' forehead crinkled as he thought. "I may be persuaded to break the lock."

"Then be persuaded, for I am in dire need of entering today." The urgency in Belle's heart poured into every word.

"Aye, your highness." Carpus bowed.

Belle followed the gardener to the gate then paced behind him as he worked on the lock. Within a minute, Carpus had the latch broken. The iron hinges grated together as the gate was forced open.

He bowed low. "The garden awaits, your highness."

Without a word, Belle slipped into the garden. The conflict in her heart only deepened as she picked her way along the overgrown paths. Mama would have never allowed the garden to reach such disarray. The rosebushes that remained were overgrown, with dead stems tangled in the growth.

She knelt and gently fingered a faded rose petal. The roses were supposed to blossom all year, yet only a few faded petals were left to fall to the ground. She plucked one of them off. That was how she felt. Like a petal clinging to its stem, hopeful of staying, fearful of being cast away.

Tears surfaced. She had been here for two weeks already, and heard no word from Papa. Percy continued to say, "cling to hope," but it was hard to hope with her birthday looming ahead, with an aunt and uncle who adored her, now begging her to return and reconsider. She reached inside her pocket and pulled out the letter. Auntie Elayne always used flowing words—words that she truly meant, starting with, "My dearest Belle..."

Now, the tears streamed freely, making the words blur before her. She had already read the letter twice, the words pulling at her heartstrings. Though Auntie Elayne said they were trying to be understanding, every paragraph urged her to come back, revealing how much they missed her.

Lord and Lady Kiralyn had treated her like a daughter. Had loved her, nurtured her, counseled her, and now, reminded her of their love. Her heart was being torn. Before she had come here, she was so sure of God's leading. Now that she was here, and everything was silent, she wasn't so sure. If God had led her here, then why must she wait? Why couldn't Papa take her into his arms, like her uncle so often did, and tell her that everything would be all right? Would he ever sit in the library with her, taking turns reading chapters of her favorite books, like Auntie Elayne did? Or would she forever be left with servants as her only companions?

One letter. That was all it would take, and Lord Kiralyn would come, settle things with Papa, and take her home—to a home where she knew she belonged. She stood and spun around to face the castle. A subtle movement in Papa's window caught her eye. She stared at it, willing her mind to stop playing tricks on her. The curtain was pulled back. She was sure it hadn't been when she entered the garden.

Her heart pounding, Belle turned back to the garden. She and Mama had stood, in this same place, day after day, admiring their secret garden. And, when Mama noticed Papa watching from his window, she would give him a bright, cheery smile, then lift Belle up, and the two would wave. What if Belle waved at Papa today? Would it evoke pleasure or wrath? She breathed deeply, calming her nerves, then peeked back at the castle. The curtain was closed.

Chapter Seven

*B*elle watched as a carriage pulled up to the front gate. Her heart seemed to pause its beating until the passenger emerged, his blond hair convincing Belle that it wasn't Lord Kiralyn, deciding to visit unannounced. She had left Lady Kiralyn's letter unanswered, her conscience smiting her every time she picked up a pen. *I shall reply on the morrow.* She had waited the past four days. Surely tomorrow she could write without any misgivings.

She turned back to her book, but her fascination with reading had waned. After only a paragraph, she returned to the window. A second carriage pulled up behind the first. Belle studied it a moment before recognizing the king's crest. The blond man came back into sight, followed by the dark-headed king. They entered their respective carriages, and the horses moved forward.

Papa was leaving. And Percy was driving him.

Slamming her book shut, Belle left it on the window seat and hurried out of the library. Her pulse quickened as she ascended the stairs. She didn't let herself stop to ask what she was doing. Instead, any prick of her conscience was hushed by her determination to press forward.

She paused at the top to ensure that Anis and Isabel were nowhere near, then ran towards the king's chambers. Without hesitation, she grasped the handle to the study door and turned. Locked, of course. She spun around to face the door to the bedchamber. It was locked as well. She closed her eyes for a moment, thinking back to the time when she was little. Aye, these were the only two doors that opened to the king's chamber.

A sliver of light shone through the edge of the bedchamber door. Belle jiggled the handle and pushed. The gap widened. She gave a slight laugh. Was it possible that Papa had neglected to order the handle changed? She dashed back to her room and burst in.

"Your highness!" Anis' reprimand was sharp. "A princess does not bolt in and out of—"

"Aye, Anis, I understand. I just need—"

"Nay, you do not understand." Anis stood in front of her, seeming to tower over her. "Lady Kiralyn gave me strict orders not to let this stay be your undoing, and I determine to please my lady. You will practice entering the chamber the proper way."

Belle backed from the room. Mayhap obeying these orders would release her from Anis' nagging sooner. Her head high, shoulders squared, Belle re-entered the room.

"Aye, much improved, your highness."

"Thank you," Belle said as she forced herself to walk, slow and sure, to her desk. Though her outward demeanor was calm, her hands betrayed nervous excitement as she fumbled for her letter opener. With the slim device in hand, she skipped out of the room.

"Your highness!" Anis' voice came after her, but the lady-in-waiting stayed in the room while Belle glided down the hallway.

Back at the bedchamber door, Belle slid the letter opener through the crack, much like she had done when she was younger. She jiggled the handle until the latch released and pushed open the door. Very little decorated the room; just the basic necessities such as a bed and washstand were present. Belle slipped through the room to the door on the next wall. The study was Papa's room, had been his special room since she was a child. The smells of leather, ink, and parchment embraced her.

She crept forward. The curtain was pulled back, allowing adequate light to filter through the window. Papa's desk was piled with books and parchments. A small shelf stood beside the desk. Belle glanced at the books. These must be Papa's special books, the ones he used regularly. She began reading the titles, trying to find something familiar—something that would remind her of when she and Papa would read together. But the long titles were not books that a father would read to his child.

On the bottom of the shelf stood a book slightly larger than the others. *Holy Bible.* Belle reached for it and eased it out. If Papa had a Bible…

Her fingers flipped the book open. The pages unfolded to the middle, where a pressed rose had been placed. A yellow rose. Standing up, Belle brought the Bible to Papa's desk and sank into his chair. She gently traced the dried petals. This must have been Mama's Bible—another token that Papa kept to remind him of her.

But the Bible is to be more than a token. Belle shut the book, the movement creating a puff of air. Paper fluttered to the floor, the slight noise causing Belle to jump. She shouldn't tarry. Placing the Bible back on the desk, she bent over to pick up the letter.

"…your careless neglect… we beseech you therefore to pass along complete guardianship… we promise to treat her as our own…"

Belle froze as her eyes skimmed the words, the meaning gradually sinking in. Lord Kiralyn had written. Papa knew the demand. And yet he said nothing. How long would it be before he said anything? Did he not care? What if he had already reached a decision?

Belle grasped the letter and read it fully. Lord Kiralyn did nothing to mask his displeasure with Papa and made no apologies for his demands. He knew what was best for Belle, more so than her own father, or so he claimed. Would Belle's future be determined by two men who barely talked to each other?

Standing, Belle clasped her mama's Bible to her heart as her eyes searched the papers that littered Papa's desk. Mayhap he had replied to Lord Kiralyn, or was in the middle of writing the reply. Anything that would give her hope that Papa wanted her. She reached forward and flipped through the loose papers, ignorant of the ones that slid to the ground. Random titles and names peppered the pages, but none of them were a response to Lord Kiralyn.

A single word erupted from the hall. Belle bolted upright, her eyes wide as she stared at the door. Papa was back so soon? The doorknob moved and a key grated into the lock. Leaving the papers scattered, Belle raced to the bedroom. She shoved the door shut so that it shielded her from the study. Papa's voice grew louder, and Belle knew his door had been opened.

"I have ordered you to call me only when duty absolutely demands my attention!"

"Your majesty..." Percy's beseeching tones were buried in the noise of paper rustling.

"That was another instance of your incompetence."

Now, while the king's tones were white-hot, would be the opportunity to slip out, yet Belle stayed. She wasn't sure what she wanted more: to simply be near Papa, or the hope that he would mention Lord Kiralyn.

"Fetch my epieu."

Belle's eyes darted to the place where the spear-like hunting weapon had always hung. It was still there.

The door swung open and Belle flattened herself against the wall. Percy bit back an exclamation when he saw her. He spun around and shut the door.

"What are you doing?" he hissed.

"'Twas just… just…" What was she doing here?

"I advise you to leave." Percy's voice sounded menacing in this low tone. "If his majesty knew you were in here…"

Percy didn't finish his warning before Belle bolted into the hall. She left the door for Percy to close, sprinting down the hall and into her room, collapsing in a chair.

"Your highness!" Anis' eyes flashed.

Belle sat up straight, realizing only then that she still clutched Mama's Bible to her chest. "I shall do better," she gasped, her heart pounding.

"You have said that before."

"Aye." But Belle wasn't talking to Anis.

Chapter Eight

The candlelight flickered as Belle sat at her desk. The blank piece of paper had been in front of her for several minutes now, but no words were written on it. The letter from Lady Kiralyn rested where she had laid it days before. She still had sent no reply.

Now, her mind composed another letter. The same thought throbbed over and over, *I miss you. I want to stay. I want to be a family again. If that will not happen, then I want to go home to Lord Kiralyn.* These torn thoughts had substanced most of her prayers. Was Percy still praying? If so, how did he pray for Papa?

Belle twisted her quill pen then dipped it again. What words would relay to Papa her love without angering him? Without causing him to force her to return? She bowed her head. *Lord, I need wisdom.*

Her pen scratched the paper, forming letters that could never communicate the yearning of her heart. One by one, the words multiplied to sentences. If she kept the letter short, perhaps Papa would read it and take it to heart.

Signing her name, Belle sprinkled the paper with sand, waited for it to dry the ink, shook the sand off, then folded the letter. She tiptoed down the hall. Her silk slippers made no noise against the stone floor, but she wanted to take no chances. Though the castle was warm this morn, her fingers felt clammy against the letter she held in her hand. She forced herself to breathe evenly as she continued up the passageway, closer to Papa's chambers.

A letter after years of silence. It seemed too stiff and formal for the bonds of family, yet there was no other way for Belle to give Papa a glimpse of her heart. She had to make an effort to reach out to Papa before it was too late.

She offered a silent prayer as she slid the letter under Papa's door. Percy would likely be the first to see it, and Belle trusted him to hand it to Papa, even if the scribe disapproved.

With her task done, Belle nearly ran back to her room. Everything was silent, except for Anis' heavy breathing. Going back to her desk, Belle opened Mama's Bible, to the verses she had read the day before. "Wait on the Lord... wait on the Lord..." the message seemed to speak from the pages over and over.

She gently closed the Bible and stood up, squinting at the clock that hung, broken and useless. She should have asked Percy to fix it already. She didn't know the time, but now that she was awake, returning to bed was useless. Instead, she donned her riding dress of hunter green which overlaid a rust under-dress. Leaving Anis sleeping in ignorance, Belle left for the stables.

Linus looked up when Belle entered. "Good morn, your royal highness. Early out, aye?"

"Aye."

"Had I known, I would have readied Galathia earlier."

"No need. I shall wait," Belle said. She went up to Keirstrider and stroked his golden coat. "How art thou, my good sir Keir?" she whispered. "Still being good to Papa? I must confess to jealousy, as you get to see him daily. I know not if I shall even speak to him again." Knowing that Papa possessed Lord Kiralyn's letter had sent a rush of urgency into her being, and it hadn't eased overnight. She patted Keirstrider in silence until Linus brought Galathia to her.

"Ride well, your highness."

"Thank you kindly, Linus." Belle let Linus help her mount then rode through the doors that he had opened.

Starting at a walk, Belle waited until they were in the field before pressing Galathia into a trot. With the horse at a slower pace, she enjoyed the morning breeze, the grass shining in the sunlight.

"Step up, Galathia!" She pushed the horse to a gallop and hid her face in Galathia's black mane. *Lord*, she prayed, s*how me what to do next. I beseech Thee, guide Papa as he reads my letter. Soften his heart and renew our relationship. My heart longs to return, yet yearns to stay. I need Thy help.* She continued praying as she rode, traveling the same route she had taken since a young child.

Turning back towards home, Belle slowed Galathia to a canter. As she neared the stables, she saw the golden horse burst out from the doors, a rider on his back. "Papa!" the word slipped from Belle's lips as she pulled Galathia to a stop.

Keirstrider thundered towards her. Belle gripped the reins tighter. Would Papa stop? Did he even see her? Closer, closer the two came, Papa's head bent down. When he was within mere yards of Belle, he looked up. For a second, his eyes locked into Belle's gaze, then Keirstrider veered to the right and galloped away.

Blinking back tears, Belle let Galathia walk forward until she reached the stables. Linus helped her down and Belle left in silence, not allowing herself to think as her feet found the path to the secret garden. Once inside, she dropped to the ground and began ripping out weeds. Today, she couldn't reflect on the progress that had been made in the past few days. Instead, her tear-blinded eyes could only see the carpet of weeds that infested the once-beautiful rose bed.

I still don't know how to befriend Papa, Lord. Had he seen her letter before his morning ride? There wasn't time to be patient. She couldn't just invite herself back into Papa's life. He had to welcome her there.

The gate creaked open and Belle forced herself to speak, "Anis, could you—"

"'Tisn't Anis, your highness."

Belle stood up at the sound of Percy's voice, blinking back the tears that she wouldn't allow to surface.

"I see you have found your way in—and made improvements."

"Aye." Belle gestured to the freshly turned soil. "It has kept my days occupied." She felt apologetic, as if trying to convince Percy that her actions were acceptable—or was she trying to convince herself? This now made two instances of her sneaking around Papa's locks.

Percy walked slowly around the garden, his hands clasped behind his back. Belle was certain that he was going to reprimand her.

"Are you happy here, your highness?"

"Happy?" Belle stuttered. When Percy nodded, she said, "I am certain God wants me here..." Was she truly certain? Her voice wavered as she continued, "Did he even read the letter I gave him this morn?"

"He received it, aye... I cannot say if it was read or not."

Belle sighed. "I keep trying to pray, like you told me to. I just... I don't know what to pray." Dropping to her knees again, she tore more weeds from the ground and whispered, "'Tisn't working." She threw aside a handful of grass and dirt.

"Did these roses bloom as soon as you and your mother planted them?" Percy's voice was next to Belle. Without looking, she knew that he knelt beside her. "Or were you that impatient little girl, dragging her mama here every morn to search for buds?"

The tears finally emerged. Percy had watched her grow up. Of course he remembered those days of impatience.

"Did you stop watering and nurturing the rosebushes just because you didn't see flowers?"

Belle shook her head and gave up on pretending to weed.

"Nay. Just like it takes time with flowers, it takes time for the Spirit's work. And you cannot give up 'watering and nurturing' because things aren't happening as quickly as you'd like them to."

"But there isn't much time!" There. She had spoken the words that haunted her.

Percy touched her elbow. "Come." He took Belle's soiled hand and led her to a bench that Carpus had repaired. The two sat in silence.

Belle didn't know how to broach the topic. Percy knew of Lord Kiralyn's letter, as he did all of the king's business. She could only assume that he knew she had seen it as well.

"I…" Belle sucked in a lungful of air. "I know of my uncle's desire."

"Is that the real reason you returned?"

"Nay!" Belle shook her head. "Mayhap it was why I returned so quickly. But I knew I needed to return."

Percy opened his mouth to talk then closed it again.

"I saw the letter," Belle blurted out. Full confession was better than pretending she knew nothing. And since she couldn't confess to Papa, she'd have to go to Percy. "It was wrong of me, I know that now. 'Twasn't my place to read it."

"Aye," Percy agreed.

Belle's hands suddenly felt damp. She pulled them away and wiped them on her skirt. "Has Papa… made a decision yet?" It was the question she wanted to ask, yet didn't want to ask.

Percy crossed his arms and leaned back. "His majesty did not say when to discuss the letter with you." He stood up, walked to one of the pruned rosebushes, and studied it silently. He looked back at Belle, his intense gaze seeming to penetrate to her thoughts. Anis would be proud at the calmness she portrayed under this pressure. Finally, Percy combed his fingers through his mostly gray hair. "I do not quite understand the king in this matter, but he says he is giving you the choice."

Belle rose and joined Percy. "What... choice?"

"The choice to go or stay. However," Percy sighed, "if you choose to go with Lord and Lady Kiralyn, you will never see your father again."

Belle knelt and jerked a weed from the ground, releasing a spray of soil. "It would not be much of a change from now." She gripped another weed and yanked.

"Belle."

Belle filled both of her hands with soil and clenched it in her fists. She loosened her fingers and watched as clumps fell back to the ground.

"Belle." Percy's voice was barely above a whisper.

Tears filled Belle's eyes again as she looked at the scribe. "I'm sorry. I am trying. It's just... it's just difficult."

"Aye, I know. But do not be weary in well doing."

He placed a gentle hand on Belle's shoulder.

The words seemed to fade into the air, but Belle's mind finished the verse, *For in due season, we shall reap, if we faint not.* Being ignored daily by Papa tempted Belle to give up. What if her efforts were not rewarded in her timetable? Would she still follow the Lord's leading?

She knew the deadline, but being reminded of it brought a shudder through her frame. "Will I ever have a chance to see my father again?"

Percy looked at the soil, fresh from Belle's attack. "Only God knows the answer to that."

Chapter Nine

*G*rede pushed at the gummy dough while Belle stood nearby, a cup of flour in her hand.

"A wee more, your highness," Grede said, looking shyly at the princess.

"I would still prefer to be the one with the dough," Belle commented as she sprinkled the flour on the mound of bread dough.

"Nay, your highness." Grede laughed nervously and shook her head. "'Tisn't seemly for the princess' hands to become soiled with such stickiness. Anis would never approve."

"Aye," Belle agreed. "But how can a meal be from me when you don't allow me to help?"

"I am uncertain how to answer, your highness." Grede shrugged her round shoulders as she shaped the dough into loaves then put them into the oven.

"Does Favian or Carpus hunt?"

"Aye, your highness."

"Have they brought pigeons in recently?"

Grede shuddered as she wiped up the table. "I despise the bird. Beg pardon, your highness."

"'Tis a pity. Papa's favorite is pigeon pie."

"For certain?"

"Aye." Belle sat on the stool. "Isabel would likely pluck the bird for you. I would like Papa's meal to be perfectly complete with all of his favorites."

Grede smiled. "Your highness, you needn't ask. A simple command will be obeyed."

"Then I command it," Belle said lightly, "but only if I may help."

"I shall try to fulfill your wish, your highness."

The two worked together in the kitchen while Isabel prepared the bird. Belle followed Grede's instructions in making pie crust, and the cook mixed the filling. As soon as it was out, Belle arranged the food carefully on the platter. Pigeon pie, broth, peas, cooked apples, nuts, cheese, and jelly. She finished with a drizzle of honey over the fresh bread. "Now I shall bring it in."

"Nay!" Grede's voice rushed out in panic. "Nay, your highness. We are never to bring his majesty's food until he asks for it."

Belle sank onto the stool and removed the apron Grede had lent her. The sound of Percy's footsteps brought her to her feet again.

"The king demands his dinner."

Belle stepped up to Percy. "The king's dinner is prepared." She gestured to the platter, laden with food.

Percy tilted his head with a half grin. "You remember?"

Belle smiled. "How could I forget? I detest pigeon pie, even though Papa tried to get me to like it." Such fond memories, when Mama was alive and Papa took every challenge with humor.

When Percy reached for the platter, Belle gripped his arm. "Nay, I shall bring it myself." How she wished one of the yellow roses had bloomed to add a spray of sunshine to her tray.

"Your highness, I cannot allow—"

"Percy, please," Belle begged.

Percy turned away slowly. "Allow me to carry the tray. 'Tis heavy."

The walk to the king's chambers had never taken so long.

"Can you walk any faster?"

Percy sighed. "I think 'tisn't a wise idea."

"Percy, 'tis time for me to see my father again."

Percy stopped and turned to face Belle. "Your highness, I do not believe you are ready to face your father."

His seriousness dampened the spark of hope Belle had nourished. She clung to the last ember and tried to appear confident. "'Tis less than a month until my birthday. 'Tis time."

Without a word, Percy turned and walked up the stairs. He continued his silence when he stopped at the king's doorway. He turned the handle. The door swung open on its hinges. Belle lifted her head and entered. Confident. With elegance. Just like Lady Kiralyn had taught her.

The king sat at his desk, his back towards the doorway. His dark, curly hair had tints of gray. His shoulders slumped, as if in perpetual defeat.

"Papa, I have brought your dinner."

The shoulders stiffened, but the king did not turn around. Belle nodded to Percy. He placed the tray slowly, soundlessly, on the desk.

"I love you, Papa, and I'm—I'm sorry for leaving you all of these years."

"Sorry enough to convince your uncle to take you completely under his wing?" The words were low, almost like a growl.

"Nay, Papa, 'tisn't like that."

"'Tisn't?" Papa finally turned. His dark brown eyes were still sharp and perceptive. He was considerably slimmer than before, and his face had aged. He studied Belle for a moment then looked up at Percy. "Percy, have you laid eyes on the Bible?" His voice was calm. Dangerously calm.

Percy looked from Belle to the king and took a deep breath.

"Answer me!" The words exploded.

"Aye, your majesty."

"And where is this Bible now?" Cold. Hard.

Belle ran forward and slipped a hand on Percy's arm. She wasn't going to let him take blame for her actions. "'Tisn't Percy's fault, Papa. I have it. 'Twas Mama's—"

"Enough!" Papa roared. Belle lost any trace of the confidence she had assumed and shrank behind Percy as Papa stood to his feet. "You came in here, without my permission. Tried to slip in without my knowledge." He walked forward, every step forcing Belle to stumble backwards. "I never asked you to return, and I certainly do not approve of this!" His fist brought the tray of food crashing to the ground. "Percy, remove her and never bring her back."

Belle didn't wait for Percy's help. She fled from the room, finding her way down the hall, more by feeling than sight as she kept the tears at bay. If Grede was in the kitchen when she sped past, she didn't see her. She continued running, through the gardens, across the field, then finally to the stables.

A sob escaped.

"Your highness?"

Belle kept her back to Linus. "Saddle my horse."

"Now? 'Tis almost dark, and a storm is brewing."

"Immediately."

Linus couldn't move fast enough for her. Sobs were churning inside her, surging as they were held back.

Linus brought Galathia to Belle. "Your highness, I cannot—"

"Shall I mount without your assistance?" Belle had never used such a sharp voice before.

"Nay, your highness." Linus bowed.

Belle avoided making eye contact as she mounted. Digging her heels into Galathia, she left the stables behind. Papa didn't want her here. He had left the choice up to her, but today, he had chosen for her. She was leaving.

Burying her head in Galathia's mane, Belle released the sobs. Before long, raindrops joined the tears on her cheeks. Still, she rode on, pushing Galathia into a gallop.

Lightning flashed, accenting the thunder that shuddered the earth. With a mad scream, Galathia reared.

The last thing Belle remembered was flying off the saddle.

Chapter Ten

The room was dark. A pinhole of light shone, then it was dark again. Belle fought against consciousness. It hurt. Everything hurt.

Voices warbled together, sometimes sounding like they were in a distant cave, other times screaming in her ear.

"Galathia..."

"Always acting afore she thinks."

"Roses..."

Then nothing.

A soft hand caressed her face. Belle tried to open her eyes, but they were too heavy. She squeezed them shut tighter. The pain wasn't so bad now.

"Belle." The deep voice was soft. Low. Subdued. "Belle, can you hear me?"

Belle opened her mouth to answer, but nothing came out.

"You shall be all right." The hand ran down her head slowly, bringing the comfort she remembered as a child. "Rest."

When she opened her eyes again, everything was blurry. She blinked and her vision cleared. The room was dimly lit—not enough to hurt her eyes. She slowly turned her head. There was a chair next to her bed, Anis sitting in it, asleep.

The clock ticked incessantly. Time was passing quickly. She needed to make her decision. Memories of Papa's hand caressing her hair flashed before her, sending warmth into her heart. Nay. Papa was angry at her. Wanted her gone. She must have been dreaming. Wishing that things had changed.

Anis moved then sat up. "Your highness," she spoke softly and tenderly, as if Belle was a babe.

"Anis." Belle's voice was raspy.

Anis brought a cup to Belle's lips and bitter liquid burned down her throat. As soon as it was gone, Belle whispered, "Bring me... writing..."

"Your highness," Anis' voice sounded strained. "You have just awoken after days. You are in no health to write a missive."

"Bring..." Belle forced her eyes open. She had to do this.

Anis moved out of sight. The time it took for her to gather Belle's writing utensils gave Belle enough rest to press on. Anis set the quill pen, ink bowl, and paper on a tray and laid it on the bed beside Belle, keeping it steady with her hand.

Still lying on her side, Belle reached for the pen. Her fingers were dry and weak as they slipped over the quill. Anis helped her to dip it in ink. One letter at a time, she wrote, "Lord Kiralyn, The king no longer desires me here. Please come." Signing her name, Belle let the pen drop.

"Send it," she whispered to Anis. Then, she was asleep again.

Chapter Eleven

ow voices awoke Belle. The room was lighter than before. It must be daytime.

"What happened?" Belle asked.

The voices stopped and footsteps came closer. Belle squinted until the forms became Anis and Isabel.

"'Tis good to see your highness awake," Isabel commented. "You caused quite a stir in the castle with your rash deeds."

"I remember the storm... the horse..." Belle's brow furrowed as she closed her eyes. Had anything happened since then?

Anis stroked her hair. "'Tis past now. The healer says you shall get well."

In the silence that fell between them, Belle realized the clock ticking. "Did Percy..." Her brow wrinkled in thought. "Did he fix the clock?"

"Nay, your highness," Isabel said. "Percy may do many things, but clocks are beyond his comprehension."

"Well then, who?"

"His majesty."

Her father… Another memory came from before the accident. "He was angry with me."

"Aye," Isabel stated.

"Why did he fix the clock?"

"Mayhap he didn't like the deathly silence while sitting in here."

"In here?" Vague memories of someone caressing her hair fought to surface then dissipated.

"Aye, your highness." Anis joined the conversation. "He rarely left your side when you slept."

"Where is he now?"

Isabel sniffed in disdain. "Percy convinced him to take some rest or we'd lose both the king and the princess."

"Help me into a gown, Anis." Belle pushed her body into a sitting position.

"Nay!" Both Anis and Isabel rushed forward to keep her from leaving the bed.

"I am well," Belle argued. "I can feel the strength in my limbs."

"You shall not be so hasty this time," Isabel reprimanded. "Your flighty ways have gotten you into this trouble. We shall not let it prolong your illness."

The door behind the maids creaked open. Anis spun around. "She's awake, your majesty."

Anis and Isabel stepped back.

"Papa." What was meant to be an exclamation came out a hoarse whisper.

"Belle." Papa hurried forward and sank into the seat beside her bed. He placed his hand on hers then, ever so slowly, squeezed it, keeping his gaze locked with Belle's. His face was grim, his deep brown eyes unreadable. "I…" He paused for a long moment. He turned and looked at the maids. "You may leave." They hurried out the room. Still, Papa didn't speak.

"Papa…"

"'T'was my fault," Papa blurted.

Belle stiffened and tried to catch her breath.

"I… was angry with you. Made you ride off."

"Papa, I forgive you," Belle breathed the words, almost inaudible.

Papa nodded and cleared his throat. "Would you like for me to read?" He tilted his head towards the bedside table, on which lay a softbound book. "We were near the end."

"I don't remember any of it," Belle whispered, not taking her eyes off Papa.

"We shall start at the beginning then." He released her hand and reached for the book. As he started, Belle kept her hand where Papa laid it. Gone was the anger she remembered possessing him, replaced by a tenderness she hadn't seen since before Mama died. She shut her eyes, relishing the moment.

Papa stopped reading. "You should rest," he said.

"Nay." Belle's eyes flew open. "Please continue." She was afraid to say more. Afraid to shatter this moment by making the wrong move.

Papa's voice was soft as he read, musically gliding up and down to fit the words. At the end of the chapter, he laid the book aside. "Are you hungry?"

Now that he asked, Belle noticed slight hunger pangs. "Aye."

"Porridge with honey?"

He remembered. Belle smiled. "Aye."

Papa left the room only to return a few minutes later with the dish. "Are you strong enough to feed yourself?"

Belle reached for the bowl. "Aye, I think so."

"Eat slowly. You've not had much food."

Belle nodded. The room was silent as she ate, taking small spoonfuls of warm porridge. After just a few bites, she handed the bowl back to Papa. "I do not think I can eat more."

Papa nodded. "You need to rest." He helped Belle lay down then covered her as she closed her eyes.

"Rest well," he said.

She thought she heard him leave the room, but then, a gentle kiss was placed on her forehead.

Chapter Twelve

Percy settled Belle in a chair surrounded by books. "There you are, your highness. His majesty shall be in shortly."

"Thank you, Percy." Belle let her hands rest in her lap. She hadn't quite gained as much strength as she thought she had when she first awoke. "Percy..."

The scribe stopped from leaving the room. "Aye?"

"Papa... is he different?" Hope laced her words. Percy would know the real answer, how the king was behind closed doors.

"Your illness worried the king."

"But did he truly change?"

Percy walked back towards Belle and knelt beside her chair. "Are you concerned he may change back, if you decide to stay?"

"Aye," Belle admitted.

"Have you considered how it might affect the king— not just you?"

Belle shifted in her seat. "What do you mean?"

"Lord and Lady Kiralyn are sincerely concerned for your well-being, yet God chose his majesty to be your father. The easier choice may be to go with Lord Kiralyn, yet who might need you more?" He stood up and walked to the door then stopped and turned. "I thought your highness had already decided."

"Nay," Belle said. "I was tempted to leave. 'Twas why I rode Galathia out."

"Anis said you wrote a letter."

"Nay! I didn't. When would I have done so?"

"When you were ill."

Belle leaned forward and laid her head in her hands. With her eyes closed, she willed herself to remember. "Percy," she murmured, not moving. "Bring Anis in."

In the moments that Percy was gone, Belle tried retracing the past few days, but everything was a dark blur. A fog she couldn't see through. As soon as she heard the quick steps of her lady-in-waiting, she demanded, "Anis, did I write a letter to Lord Kiralyn when I was ill?"

"Aye, your highness."

The words set Belle's heart racing. "Did you send the letter?" She wished that, this once, her lady-in-waiting would have done something against her orders.

"Aye, your highness."

Anis' affirmation felt like a knife cutting at her heart. Her head began pounding. "When?"

Anis didn't meet Belle's gaze. "I took great liberty, your highness. I knew his majesty was afraid of losing you. And if you were gone, what good would the letter do for Lord Kiralyn?"

"So you didn't send it?" Belle couldn't keep excitement from lacing her words.

"I sent it, your highness." Belle's hopes were dashed with Anis' admission. "But not until you awoke yestermorn."

Belle turned to Percy. "How long does it take for a missive to reach Lord Kiralyn?"

"By route, two days."

Two days? If he left as soon as he received it, he would be here on the morrow. "How long would it take you to bring one?"

"If you lend me Galathia, I could take the forest route and be there by morn."

"Bring me my writing things," Belle ordered Anis.

The lady-in-waiting's eyes hardened. "You have made your decision, your highness."

"Nay!" Belle cried. "I was ill." She shuddered at the real reason it bothered her. She knew that she hadn't sought God before writing the letter. What repercussions would it have?

"The lord and lady would treat you well," Anis argued. "Much better than this beast."

Belle rose on shaking legs. "Do not disrespect my father, Anis. I could have you sent off."

Percy stood beside Belle, steadying her. "Anis, you have heard her highness' orders. Retrieve her writing utensils." He waited until Anis stormed out of the room before helping Belle back to her seat. "I shall ready Galathia and return."

"Papa won't be angry with you leaving?"

Percy lifted half of his mouth in a grin. "His majesty will overcome his anger with me. You haven't long before he comes in. You best hurry."

Belle watched Percy leave, every limb aching to get up and run to her room herself instead of waiting on her sullen maid to go for her.

The door reopened and Belle looked up expectantly. Her breath caught as Papa slipped in. *Not yet.* She tried to rise, but Papa shook his head. "Nay, stay there." He brought a chair next to her and picked up the book. "Shall we resume?"

Belle tried to mirror his smile, but her mouth went dry. How could she write such a vital message in his presence? Her head throbbed harder. The vowels and consonants blurred together, making no sense as Papa read. She could excuse herself for weariness, but it would come at the cost of forfeiting her time with Papa today— and such a choice might cost her more than she was willing to pay.

When Anis stepped into the room, her smile was smug. She laid Belle's writing pouch on a shelf, gave a slight curtsy, then left.

"Is something the matter?"

Belle hadn't noticed when Papa ended the chapter. "Nay," she lied. She attempted to smile. "You may continue."

The reading that had been a soothing balm yesterday now filled Belle with anxiety.

"Gala—" Percy stopped and looked from the king to Belle. She gave him a look of misery. It must have conveyed the message she implored because he clicked his heels together and cleared his throat. "Your majesty."

Papa stopped reading with a low growl. "Percy, can you not see I am occupied?"

"Aye, your majesty. I usually would not interrupt, but there is a pressing need which requires your immediate attention."

Papa slammed the book shut. "You must be certain of that."

"Aye, your majesty." Percy looked grave as he bowed.

Papa stood. "I shall be back." His voice was stern, but Belle knew the sternness was directed at his servant.

"Percy, send Anis in."

"Aye, your highness." He bowed again. "It shall not be long." The slight nod he added to his words told Belle that he was urging her to hurry.

The door shut and Belle stood to her feet. She had been kept from walking any distance since her accident, but there wasn't time to wait for Anis. Belle grasped for the bookshelf that lined the wall. Gripping the shelf, she slid one foot in front of the other. Then again. Her knees threatened to buckle. She stopped and sucked in a staggering breath. *Lord, I made a big mistake; please help me to undo it. Give me strength to reach my pouch.* She tried again. One foot. Then the next. As she inched forward, she formulated the letter in her mind. "Lord Kiralyn, I was mistaken in my last missive. I have decided to stay." She took a few more steps. Paused to catch her breath. "Nothing you say will change my mind. Please do not come. I am certain God would have me to stay here."

Collapsing on the floor, Belle stretched towards her pouch, gripping a string. It tumbled to the ground, contents scattering. Gathering the pen and ink, she placed the paper on the floor. Her fingers shook as she formed the first letter. It couldn't look like she was hesitant about this message. She stopped and forced herself to relax. To breathe in, then out. Dipping the pen, she tried again. This time, the letters were smooth and bold.

"Your highness!"

"Anis, leave me be," Belle ordered, dipping her pen again. She wrote swiftly, not letting herself stop again until the letter was finished. Her fingers started shaking as she sprinkled sand on the paper. Dumping it clean, she folded it and handed it to Anis. "Give this to Percy." She locked eyes with Anis. "I am trusting you to follow this command."

Anis nodded without a word then stooped to help Belle up.

"Leave me be. Papa cannot see that you have a missive. I will return to the chair. Just take the letter to Percy."

Belle waited until Anis left the room then scooped the writing utensils back into the bag. Now, she could only pray that Percy was fast enough.

Chapter Thirteen

What had she done? The letter written during her illness plagued Belle as she tossed in bed. Even now, Percy was probably riding hard towards Kiralyn in an attempt to undo her choice. Would he arrive before the lord left? Belle could only pray that the timing was right.

She watched as layers of purples and gold shifted in the sky with the sunrise. Sitting up, Belle awoke Anis.

"Bring me my blue gown," she asked.

"Your highness, 'tis important for you to have as much sleep as possible, with your recent injury."

Belle held back her retort. If only Anis knew how little she had slept. "I am awake and shan't be sleeping anymore. My dress, please."

Anis grumbled as she laid out the royal blue garment. Belle fingered the smooth silk before Anis helped her into the gown.

"I would like to go to the library, Anis."

"I cannot call Percy. You have sent him away." Anis' voice was hard.

"Aye," Belle agreed slowly. "Favian will have to do then."

"Aye, your highness."

Once she was settled in the library she calmed her mind from the wild rambling it had taken during the night. She couldn't leave. How could she have been so blind? If she left, would it help her father to know Christ? In her focus on personal comfort, she had forgotten about eternal values. Following God here did not mean that she would embrace a lifestyle of comfort. Instead, she would find the purpose He had for her. To run away to Lord Kiralyn's would only be to fail Jesus Christ.

"Have you solved the kingdom's problems?" Papa's voice was light, almost in jest.

Belle looked up at him. "Nay, but mayhap I have solved my own. Good morn."

"Have you broken your fast?"

"Nay."

"Shall we go—"

The door thumped open, interrupting them. "Your majesty." Favian bowed low. "Lord Kiralyn to see you."

"Lord Kiralyn?" Papa's back straightened. Gone was any tenderness from the moment before. "He is not welcome in my castle."

"I should think not," Lord Kiralyn said as he walked in. "But, seeing as your daughter is not welcomed either, I shall soon rid you of both our presences."

"Nay," Belle cried, scrambling to her feet. She stood beside Papa. "I was ill when I wrote—"

"You wrote?" Papa roared.

"I was ill."

"You went behind my back again?" Papa stepped closer to Belle. She stumbled backwards. "You said not a word to me about writing."

"Aye, I had forgotten."

"Forgotten? Likely excuse!"

"I want to stay." Belle refused to back down, though her body began trembling from weakness.

Lord Kiralyn stepped beside Belle. "You cannot stay with a—a madman like him."

"Is that all I am to you?" the king shouted at Lord Kiralyn. "You think I do not know a thing. You think you're the only one who knows what is best. I am her father, Raoul."

"Aye," Lord Kiralyn hissed. "Her father that never looked out for her well-being."

"I gave her a choice."

Lord Kiralyn reached into his pocket and pulled out the missive Belle had written. "She told me her choice."

Belle looked at her father, expecting to see the rage with which she had become familiar. Instead, she saw sorrow. Pain. Betrayal.

Silence roared in her ears as Papa looked from her to Lord Kiralyn, then back to her.

"Take her then," his voice was firm as steel. "But she will never return." His brown eyes hardened. "She is no longer considered my daughter." His footsteps pounded as he turned from Belle and disappeared out the door.

Chapter Fourteen

"You cannot convince me," Belle whispered. She sank into the chair. "I sent another missive by Percy."

"You asked me to come." The gentleness in Lord Kiralyn's voice brought tears to Belle's eyes. He had been like a father to her, when her own father wasn't there. He was willing to assume legal responsibility of her, without making her promise to give anything in return.

"I love you and Auntie Elayne. You have done so much for me, but I need to stay here now."

Lord Kiralyn paced the floor in front of her. "You are not wanted here, Belle. What kind of life would you live? One of seclusion? What about your future?"

"I do not know, but I'm trusting that God knows what He is doing. He led me here. To leave Papa now would be to disobey God."

"That was not the tenor the letter."

"Aye," Belle agreed. "'T'was wrong of me to write it. I did not seek God afore writing it." She lowered her voice. "Mayhap..." She hesitated. "Mayhap, if we keep praying, Papa's heart will change and he'll let me return... for a visit."

The frown on Lord Kiralyn's face tore at Belle's heart. In only a few moments, she had caused pain to both the men she loved.

"You are certain?"

"Aye." She was more certain this instant than ever before, though her heart felt like it was shredding.

Lord Kiralyn stopped pacing. "You are certain?" he repeated. This time, he searched Belle's face as he asked the question.

Belle nodded. "I have thought it through. Prayed it through. I am decided."

Her uncle said nothing for a long moment then bowed his head. "'Twill be too late for a proper debut if you change your mind at a later date."

"Aye, I understand."

"Well, you always have a home with us." Lord Kiralyn squeezed Belle's hand and helped her to her feet. "I suppose I shall have to say farewell?"

Belle smiled through her tears. "Send Auntie Elayne my love." She rose to her toes and placed a gentle kiss on her uncle's cheek. "And tell her I shall write."

"Aye. God be with you." Lord Kiralyn walked to the door where Favian still stood.

Belle stepped forward. "Favian. I need your assistance."

Favian looked from Lord Kiralyn to the princess. "Yes, your highness."

"Take me to the garden," she requested. "The secret garden." She needed time alone. Alone in a place where the world's sorrows and cares seemed erased.

As they traveled through the castle, Belle prepared herself for what she might find. A garden left to itself for more than a few days would undo the work that she had put into it.

"You may set me down here," she said as Favian brought her to the end of the knot garden. Once on her feet, she closed her eyes and took a deep breath. She would start again, working at the weeds, removing that which had marred her work. She had a second chance with this, just like God had given her a second chance with her father.

Taking a step forward, Belle pushed the gate open. Instead of weeds, the soil was freshly turned, the paths neat, and roses budding and blossoming. A small smile crossed Belle's face. Carpus kept the garden in shape— even better than when she, herself had tended it.

She walked up towards the largest rosebush. Leaves now covered it, giving proof that it was alive. If only she knew the color of the rose—if it was Mama's rose.

"You didn't leave."

Belle spun around at the sound of Papa's voice behind her. "I told you I couldn't."

"Why did you stay?"

Belle took a step forward. "Because you are my father. And… I love you." Another step forward. How long would it take for the years of hardness to fade away? "God entrusted me to you, and I know He wants me to stay. I'm not leaving, Papa."

The king nodded then took his hands from behind his back. There, in his grasp, nestled a yellow rose. Even in the gray morn, it seemed to shine brightly.

"'Tis her yellow rose," he said, taking a step closer.

"Aye," Belle agreed, nodding as tears coursed down her cheeks. She closed the gap between her and Papa. "'Twas you who tended the garden, while I was sick, was it not?"

"Aye." Papa held the rose out to Belle.

"A ray of sunshine," Belle murmured, reaching out her finger and touching a petal.

"Like a beacon of hope. I… I didn't think that I would ever see that beacon again." He paused and placed the rose in Belle's hand. "But you've given it to me. I want to know why." He lifted her in his strong arms and brought her to a bench. He set her down gently then wrapped his arms around her.

Belle smiled and leaned her head against Papa's chest. "I would love to tell you."

The End

Discussion Questions

Chapter One

- Why do you think Belle returned to the castle?
- How would you feel, returning to a place you hadn't been in years?

Chapter Two

- How do you think Belle felt, her first time back at the castle?
- How would you feel if someone you cared for refused to see you?

Chapter Three

- What changes did Belle face as she returned?
- What difficult changes have you had to grow through?

Chapter Four

- Why was the garden a special place for Belle?
- What do you do when your heart is full of sorrow?

Chapter Five

- What sin came to Belle's mind when she realized that she was a sinner? Why would this "small" sin make her guilty before

God? Can you think of any verses that would support your answer?

- Like Belle, every human on earth is guilty of sinning before God. Have you accepted Jesus Christ's forgiveness for your sins?

Chapter Six

- Was it right for Belle to enter the garden her father had locked? Why or why not?

- Have you ever had a hard choice to make? Did you take it to the Lord in prayer?

Chapter Seven

- Was Belle right in entering her father's room without his permission? Why or why not?

- What did Belle take back from Papa's room? Why?

- Have you ever done something, then immediately realize you shouldn't have done it?

Chapter Eight

- Ultimately, to whom did Belle turn for help?

- What encouragement did Percy offer Belle?

- Is there any area in your life in which you're tempted to be weary in well-doing? How can you continue and not faint?

Chapter Nine

- How did Belle find a way to reach her Papa? How did he respond?

- In what ways can you reach out to those around you in love— even if they may not respond well?

Chapter Ten

- What was Belle's rash decision? Even though she was sick, was it right for her to make that decision? Why or why not?

Chapter Eleven

- How did Papa now reach out to Belle? How do you think she felt about this turn of events?
- The start to mending any relationship is forgiveness. Is there anyone in your life that you are keeping at a distance because of unforgiveness in your heart?

Chapter Twelve

- When Belle realized that she had done wrong, what did she then do?
- Do you take quick action to remedy mistakes that you have made?

Chapter Thirteen

- What did Belle finally come to realize in her decision about staying with Papa?
- When you make decisions, do you usually base them off of your own comfort? Or do you strive to follow God and His eternal purposes?

Chapter Fourteen

- How did Belle's decision affect Papa?
- Has God ever given you a second chance with someone or something? How did you take advantage of that second chance?

Historical Note

Though *Befriending the Beast* is a work of fiction in a castle and land created from my own imagination, I have based my research on medieval England. Therefore, the meals that were eaten, the herb and knot gardens, and rooms mentioned are all things that would have been relevant to a medieval castle.

Another point of interest is the language. I did not extensively research correct dialogue for the era, but I did try my best to portray words and language to bring in the aura of the time period, yet still make it easy for the modern reader to enjoy.

Keirstrider would be my "fairytale twist," as I doubt there is a fantastic gold horse with blue eyes in history. But the story wouldn't be complete (in my imagination) without him!

Author's Note

One night, a question popped into my mind: "What if the beast was Belle's father?" I wasn't even considering ways to rewrite fairytales, but I jotted that question down and wondered if a story would come of it. Little did I know that in less than three months, my new "short story idea" would turn into a novella—*and* be ready for publication.

First and foremost, I praise the Lord. He not only gave me this idea, but He also He allowed me time and creativity to write the story. He provided a meaningful message to interweave into the story, and He also sent the right people for the right time to help this story become what it is today.

One person stands out as being very instrumental to the development of this story: Anita Heath. For my 7,800-word rough draft, you gave me 5,139 words of suggestions, critiques, and pointers. Yeah. The following drafts were SO much richer because of your input! I can't thank you enough for all of the time you took out of your own writing priorities to help me out!

And then there are my other "first readers" who suffered through that poor, very rough, first-draft and offered their suggestions. Joan Bolen, Kenzi, Janell Rogers, Temperance Johnson, Kimberly Villalva, thank you so much for encouraging me to keep going with Belle's unique story!

Now, for my beta-readers. Those who read a more final draft yet added some great suggestions to refine it even more. Thank you, Kellyn Roth, Amanda Leite, Salinn Bethany, Nicole Acquah, Janell Rogers, Kenzi, Kimberly Snyder, Liberty Bluebelle, Liberty Baehr, Amanda Talkington, Katie Hamilton, Jesseca Wheaton, and Deborah Dunson.

Not on the above list is my family. Mom, Elizabeth, Rachel, Joanna, and Naomi all read *Befriending the Beast* at one point and time and either offered valuable tips or just warmed my heart with their enthusiastic support.

Aimee Hebert, though this book was written for you, you still helped me in looking up things in my medieval books. Thanks for helping with your book.

Kenzi, your helping in looking over the discussion questions was much-needed and much-appreciated! Thank you.

There is a group of people out there who have read my short stories and *Journey to Love,* and have, in turn, encouraged and prompted me to keep on writing. Unless you're an author, you really won't know *how* much of a blessing your support is! So, even though I may not know you by name, I've read your reviews and have been encouraged. Thanks!

As with every book I finish, it is hard to stop and think of the many people who were a part of its success. If I missed someone, I truly am sorry. It's not that you weren't helpful, but that my memory is on the verge of pathetic.

Now, as we close another adventure, I am eagerly awaiting what the Lord has in store for me! But, until then, I pray that God uses Belle and her story to be a help to someone out there.

By God's grace,

Amanda Tero

~ Other Works by Amanda Tero ~

Orphan Journeys Novellas
Journey to Love (Marie's Story, 1901)

Orphan Journeys Short Stories
Letter of Love (Edward's Story, 1902)

Short Stories
Coffee Cake Days

Deb's Bible (for new readers)

Debt of Mercy

Letters from a Scatter-brained Sister

Maggie's Hope Chest

Noelle's Gift

Peace, Be Still

Found on Amazon and www.amandatero.com

CONNECT WITH AMANDA

Email: amandaterobooks@gmail.com
Website: www.amandatero.com
Facebook: www.facebook.com/amandaterobooks
Instagram: amandateroauthor
Pinterest: amandaruthtero
Blog: www.withajoyfulnoise.blogspot.com
Goodreads: AmandaTero

HAVE YOU MET THE MASTER AUTHOR?

The "author and finisher of our faith," the "author of salvation?"

Well, why do we need to know the Master Author?

There is no man, woman, boy, or girl who is without sin. Romans 3:23 says, "For **all** have sinned, and come short of the glory of God;"

Have you lied, cheated, stolen, taken God's Name in vain, coveted, or lusted? All of these are sins according to God's Holy law (see Exodus 20). Even if we neglect in just one area of God's law, we are found sinners. "For whosoever shall keep the whole law, and yet offend in one point, he is guilty of all." (James 2:10) The payment for sin is death ("For the wages of sin is death;" Romans 6:23a)

God does not desire to leave us in this hopeless, destitute state. He did what we could not do and paid the debt for us. He sent His Son, Jesus Christ, to come, be born of a virgin, live a sinless, perfect life, die a cruel death, and rise again, victorious over sin, death, and hell! Romans 6:23 continues to say, "but the gift of God is eternal life through Jesus Christ our Lord." Jesus Christ is the only way to have eternal life, to be forgiven ("Jesus saith unto him, I am the way, the truth, and the life: no man cometh unto the Father, but by me." John 14:6). God promised us that, "If we confess our sins, He is faithful and just to forgive us our sins, and to cleanse us from all unrighteousness." (1 John 1:9)

Salvation comes by putting your faith and trust in Jesus Christ for salvation and eternity ("Believe on the Lord

Jesus Christ, and thou shalt be saved, " Acts 16:31) and repenting from our sins ("Repent ye therefore, and be converted, that your sins may be blotted out," Acts 3:19).

So, have you met the Author?

Made in the USA
Columbia, SC
05 September 2019